Contents

There's Something Down There!

You know when someone says, "Just ignore me!" or "Pretend I'm not here!" and you obviously CAN'T do either of those things. And you ESPECIALLY CAN'T when it's your HEAD TEACHER and he's CONSTANTLY coming into your classroom and looking in

1

all the cupboards or CRAWLING ALONG THE CORRIDOR or doing loads of

SILENT CRYING.

Well, that all happened to US at our school, and it's how we knew that something

STRANGE

was going on.

We all knew that Mr Graves must be LOOKING FOR SOMETHING but it was when Gary Petrie's DAD said that he saw something SHINY in the SCHOOL BASEMENT that EVERYTHING CHANGED.

And it was when we sent CHEESE AND ONION down to the basement on a

SECRET MISSION

wearing a CAMERA that everything CHANGED AGAIN.

And NONE of us could BELIEVE what we saw when we watched the FOOTAGE.

Maisie said that we should forget ALL ABOUT IT and NEVER go near the basement again.

But then we heard WAILING and SCREECHING when we were in class and Jodi said that ACTION WAS NEEDED. And that's when things got SERIOUS. And very, VERY smelly.

Is Mr Graves Crying?!

One day when we were in class, our head teacher, Mr Graves, rushed into our classroom and said, "Just ignore me!", and then he started opening ALL the cupboards REALLY FAST and looking inside.

That's when our teacher, Miss Jones, asked

Mr Graves if he was OK, and he nodded and said that he was, even though he definitely wasn't acting like he was OK and he was EMPTYING everything out of the cupboards and on to the floor.

That's when Jodi leaned over the table and whispered, "What's he looking for?"

I just shrugged, because it was obvious he

was looking for something but I had

what it could be.

Then at break we saw Mr Graves **CRAWLING** along the corridor, and when he saw us he just crawled **REALLY FAST** into his office and shut the door behind him.

None of us knew what to do because it's really hard to know **WHAT** to do when your head teacher starts crawling along the ground like a baby. So we didn't do anything.

But then at assembly the next morning Mr Graves started doing

SILENT CRYING

while he was telling us about the **NEW SCHOOL DINNERS MENU.**

At first I thought maybe he was crying because the **DINNER LADIES** had made a new, worse **SHEPHERD'S PIE** (because the shepherd's pie at our school is disgusting!).

But they hadn't. And the new menu sounded quite

GOOD

actually, so it didn't make any sense that Mr Graves was crying about it.

We all sat there STARING at Mr Graves as he talked about the VEGAN SAUSAGES with TEARS running down his face.

The teachers were looking at each other all confused, so it was obvious that they didn't know what was going on either.

That's when Zach said, "Should we do something? Should we get the nurse?"

But Jodi said, "SHHHHH!", and then she leaned forward and NARROWED her eyes and STARED at Mr Graves. And we knew that she was trying to READ HIS THOUGHTS because Jodi says that she wants to be the type of POLICE OFFICER who can

GET INSIDE PEOPLE'S HEADS

and make criminals tell her EVERYTHING

so she can solve all the CRIMES.

Then Mr Graves stopped telling us about the VEGAN SAUSAGES and started telling us that the GRASS in the playground was getting cut on Friday and that's when he REALLY started crying and SNIFFING loads.

Zach said that maybe Mr Graves was crying because he had

EXTREME HAY FEVER

that made him cry even when he was only TALKING about grass.

But then Jodi looked at Zach and said, "Zach, that's ridiculous."

And Zach said, "Is it?"

And Jodi said, "Yes."

And Zach said, "IS IT?"

And Jodi said, "YES."

But before Zach could say "IS IT?" again, Mr Graves ran off the stage!

Turn That Music Down!

The next day, when we got to school, there was a **VAN** parked outside the school doors and it had **LOUD MUSIC** coming out of it and someone was singing along **REALLY BADLY**.

Me and Jodi and Zach tried to get past,

but the van was BLOCKING the stairs that go up to the BIG DOORS.

So that's when Jodi went up and KNOCKED on the van doors, and when they opened we all

GASPED

because it was GARY PETRIE from our class.

And Gary said, "YOU RAAAANG?!"

Gary Petrie always says ANNOYING things like that instead of just normal stuff like "hello" or "what do you want?"

So that's when Jodi started explaining that we couldn't get into the school because the van was BLOCKING the steps, but Gary just said, "WHAT? I CAN'T HEAR YOU!" because the music was too loud and someone in the back of the van was singing even LOUDER and WORSE than before.

So Jodi shouted, "I SAID, MOVE YOUR VAN!"

And that's when the music suddenly stopped and someone ELSE appeared from inside the van that looked EXACTLY like Gary except older and COMPLETELY BALD.

The man looked at us and said, "And who are you lot? The police?!"

Then he laughed really loud and he sounded JUST like Gary does when he laughs.

That's when Gary started laughing too and said, "Nah. They're just my friends, Dad."

I looked at Jodi and she looked at me because I wouldn't exactly call Gary our FRIEND because mostly he just makes FUN of us or does stuff to ANNOY us. And Jodi and Gary DEFINITELY don't get along.

That's when Gary's dad wiped his hands on his overalls and jumped out of the van.

And for a second I thought that he'd landed on his **KNEES** because he was almost the same height as me! But then I remembered that Gary's small too, so that made sense.

Gary's dad looked right at **ME** and said, "You must be Gary's girlfriend! Nice to meet you."

Everyone **GASPED**, and I shouted, "**WHAT?!**" because I **DEFINITELY** wasn't Gary's girlfriend and I had

why he was saying that I was.

But then Gary's dad burst out laughing again and said, "Don't have kittens, lass! I'm only pulling your leg!" And then he slapped his **OWN** leg and laughed again for ages, even though it **DEFINITELY** wasn't funny.

That's when Mr Graves appeared and we all thought that he was going to tell Gary's dad to move his van but he **DIDN'T**.

He just rushed over and said, "Mr Petrie, thank goodness you're here! Come with me, please. Quickly!" And then he ran off round the side of the school.

Gary's dad looked a bit surprised and then he grabbed his tool bag and said, "Must be a real emergency! See you later, kiddo." And then he gave Gary a high five and rushed after Mr Graves.

I looked at Jodi and I thought that she was going to be FURIOUS because the van was still blocking the stairs.

But she WASN'T furious.

She was SMILING.

And then she said, "It's time to find out what's going on with Mr Graves. Follow me!"

Follow Me, Amigos!

There was **NO WAY** to shake off Gary Petrie. He followed us round the back of the school where we'd seen Mr Graves and Gary's dad disappear behind a wall.

But when we turned the corner they were gone.

Jodi looked at us with a

on her face. And then she said, "Where did they go?! They've disappeared!"

That's when Gary Petrie LAUGHED and said, "I know."

Jodi took a DEEP BREATH and made her ARMS and HANDS and FINGERS go really STRAIGHT and TIGHT and then she said, "OK. Where did they go?"

But Gary just SMILED an ANNOYING SMILE and began stroking his CHIN like he

had an IMAGINARY BEARD or something.

I looked at Jodi, but she didn't look back because she had her eyes closed tight in ANGER and I could see that her ARMS were actually SHAKING.

So that's when I said, "What do you want, Gary?"

And Zach said, "Yeah, Gary. Name your PRICE."

Because it was OBVIOUS that Gary WANTED something in return for telling us where Mr Graves and his dad had disappeared to.

And that's when Gary said, "I want IN."

And as **SOON** as he said that Jodi's eyes **SHOT OPEN** and she said,

"NO WAY!"

And Gary said, "**WAY!**"

And Jodi shouted, "**NEVER!**"

I looked at Zach and he put his head in his hands and I knew that he did it because this was going to go on **FOREVER** because there was **NO WAY** Jodi was going to give Gary what he wanted. Because what Gary wanted was to be part of our **INVESTIGATION**.

But then, all of a sudden, Jodi's face

CHANGED and she said, "OK. You're in."

And me and Zach

GASPED.

Because Jodi NEVER gives in.

And then she said, "Take us to them, Gary."

And Gary nodded and said, "Follow me, amigos!"

Gary made us follow him and hide in a bush round the back of the school that was

OUT OF BOUNDS for pupils.

My heart was POUNDING because I knew that if we got caught there, we'd be in BIG TROUBLE.

Then Gary said, "Do you see that over there?"

So we all looked at where Gary was pointing and there was some sort of HOLE in the ground next to the wall.

We asked what it was, but Gary just smiled an ANNOYING SMILE and said, "Just wait. You'll see."

So we waited. And waited. And WAITED.

And then eventually we saw Mr Graves and Gary's dad COME OUT of the hole!

And then Mr Graves pulled two doors shut over the hole and they both walked away.

We all STARED at each other.

Then Zach said, "What was THAT?!"

Gary turned to us with a huge grin on his face and said, "None of you had any idea where they'd gone but I KNEW. And THAT is why I am now in charge of this investigation!"

I thought Jodi was going to explode. But she didn't. But she definitely looked like she WANTED TO. But I knew that she was keeping her anger INSIDE and letting Gary help us for the SAKE OF THE

INVESTIGATION.

Then Gary said that HE had been doing his OWN investigation into why Mr Graves was acting so WEIRD and that it was time to

JOIN FORCES,

but that he would still be the one in charge.

And then he grinned at Jodi because he KNEW FINE WELL that he was annoying her. But Jodi just fake-smiled back and said, "Is there anything else?"

And Gary said, "Yes. I've been watching Mr Graves since he started acting WEIRD

and I've seen him go in there LOADS."

Zach said that maybe the door was a

SECRET PASSAGEWAY

that led to Mr Graves's office and that THAT

was why this part of the playground was

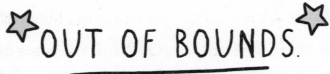

OUT OF BOUNDS.

But then Gary laughed his ANNOYING

LAUGH and said, "TRY AGAIN!"

So that's when I said, "You obviously know

what it is, so just tell us, Gary."

But Gary didn't answer. He just got up and started SNEAK-WALKING over to the little door, so we followed him.

We watched as Gary put one hand on the door and the other hand on his HIP and said, "THIS, ladies and gentlemen, is the SECRET DOOR."

We all STARED at the door, and I thought that it was probably HUNDREDS of years old because it was all faded and a bit CREEPY.

That's when Jodi said, "I can't believe this! How long have you known about this secret door, Gary? You should have told us!"

And I knew that Jodi had said that because

Gary KNEW that we dealt with LOADS of

SECRET
INVESTIGATIONS

at our school, like the time with the VAMPIRE RATS and the DEMON DINNER LADIES, and that we OBVIOUSLY needed to know about any

SECRET DOORS

so that we could do our investigations properly and save our school each time.

That's when Gary did the annoying imaginary BEARD thing again and said, "There's a LOT of stuff I know that you don't."

And Jodi's EYES went WIDE.

Then Gary said, "Like, did you know that these doors lead to a huge BASEMENT?"

And we all GASPED again because we definitely DIDN'T know that.

So I said, "Wait. You're telling us our school

has a

BASEMENT!?.

And Gary GRINNED and said, "YUP."

Me and Zach and Jodi all STARED at each

other because this was

BIG.

And then Gary GRINNED even wider and

said, "And there's MORE."

Jodi's eyes looked like they were going

to BURST. That's how wide they were.

And she leaned towards Gary and did her **MIND-READING STARE** and said, "Tell us everything. Now!"

But Gary just laughed and said, "One thing at a time, my dear. One thing at a time."

And then before Jodi could say anything back, Gary unhooked the **LATCH** on the

SECRET DOOR

and **OPENED IT.**

We all peered inside and saw a **WOODEN STAIRCASE** that went down to the **BASEMENT.**

Then before any of us could ask any more questions, Gary said, "So … are we all agreed I'll be taking the lead on this investigation?"

And before any of us could answer, Gary zipped his coat up and disappeared down the stairs.

The Secret Basement

We all **JUMPED** out of our skin when a voice from behind us yelled, "What are you doing over there?"

It was our teacher, Miss Jones, rushing towards us from the other side of the playground.

That's when Zach looked at the OPEN DOORS and then he looked at us. Because we knew that we were already in DEEP TROUBLE for being in an

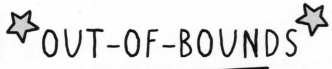

OUT-OF-BOUNDS

area and that we'd probably get EXPELLED for going near the BASEMENT too.

And that's when Gary's head appeared and he said, "Go! SAVE YOURSELVES! I'll be OK." And then he pulled the doors shut so Miss Jones wouldn't see.

I GULPED because I knew that Gary was

probably in

COMPLETE DARKNESS

down there!

Miss Jones stopped halfway across the playground and yelled, "The bell's gone! You know you're not allowed in that part of the playground! What are you doing?"

So Jodi yelled back, "SORRY, MISS! WE DIDN'T HEAR IT!"

And then Zach yelled, "WE WERE FOLLOWING A SPIDER, MISS. IT'S GOT NINE LEGS, WHICH IS WEIRD

BECAUSE SPIDERS USUALLY ONLY HAVE EIGHT LEGS. SO THAT'S WHY WE WERE FOLLOWING IT."

Jodi closed her eyes and shook her head, because Zach is probably the **WORST** liar that you get.

That's when Miss Jones started walking towards us **REALLY FAST**, and Jodi hissed, "Zach! Look what you've done! She knows we're up to something now!"

So I said that we should run towards Miss Jones really fast, so we did. And when we got to her she gave us all a bit of a **LOOK**. And then she looked over to the place where

we'd been standing.

So that's when Jodi said, "Is that Mr Graves over there, Miss?"

And then she pointed behind Miss Jones even though there was no one there.

And then when Miss Jones looked, Jodi said, "Oh, he was waving at you, I think. But he's gone now."

And it TOTALLY WORKED. Miss Jones stopped looking at us suspiciously and said, "Come on. The bell went five minutes ago."

So we all rushed off with Miss Jones.

And I was the last one to turn the corner, so just before I did I looked back to see if

Gary was opening the doors.

But he wasn't.

And that's when I remembered THE LATCH.

The latch was on the

OUTSIDE.

And that's when I started to worry that the latch might have closed accidentally when Gary shut the doors.

And that Gary might be TRAPPED in the DARK BASEMENT!!!

None of us could concentrate on our maths because every time someone walked past the classroom door we

GASPED

because we were hoping it was GARY.

That's when Maisie said, "Why are you all being so weird? Is something wrong?"

And then Maisie's eyes went WIDE and she said, "Oh no. Something IS wrong, isn't it? What is it?! Tell me!"

But before we could even say ONE WORD the WHOLE TABLE started to SHAKE.

So that's when Zach told Maisie what had happened with the BIG VAN and Gary's DAD and the EMERGENCY and finding the SECRET DOOR.

But then he stopped and looked at Jodi. And Jodi shook her head a TINY bit, which most people probably wouldn't even NOTICE. But me and Zach notice because it's a SECRET-SIGNAL THING and it means that we shouldn't tell Maisie something yet (or maybe ever!) because she'll probably find it TOO SCARY and faint INSTANTLY.

But then Maisie said, "I saw that, Jodi."

And we

because we didn't **KNOW** that Maisie knew about the signal.

So that's when Jodi took a deep breath and said, "Gary went into the basement."

And Maisie **SQUEAKED** and the table started shaking **SO MUCH** then that me and Zach had to use **BOTH HANDS** to keep it **STABLE**.

That's when Miss Jones walked past our table **REALLY SLOWLY** to see if we were doing what we were SUPPOSED to be doing and we all FAKE-SMILED and tried to hold the table as TIGHTLY as we could so the pens would stop SHAKING in the tub.

Miss Jones LINGERED for a bit and then she moved on to the next table. And that's when Maisie said, "What happened to him? Tell me. I can take it."

I knew that I wasn't going to be the one to tell her that Gary might be trapped in the DARK BASEMENT, because, to be honest, I didn't think that Maisie COULD take it.

So I looked at Jodi and she gave me a LOOK as if to say that I should be the one to tell Maisie. So I gave Jodi a LOOK RIGHT BACK.

So that's when Jodi took a deep breath and said, "Maisie, it was an accident. Gary shut the basement doors and told us to save ourselves. We thought he'd have crawled out by now, but we think the latch might have accidentally closed so we're going back at break to get him. It's going to be OK."

And that's when Maisie started

SCREAMING.

Locked In!

Maisie wouldn't stop SCREAMING. And she screamed SO LOUD that Miss Jones ran for help because she thought Maisie must have been stung by a WASP.

We all watched as Maisie got taken away to the NURSE and then listened as her screams got quieter and quieter as she was carried further away down the corridor.

That's when Zach said, "We definitely shouldn't have told her."

And I nodded because I don't think I have EVER heard Maisie scream so loud.

So as SOON as the bell went for break we RAN outside and round to the back of the school and opened the basement doors.

I was hoping that Gary would be RIGHT THERE, waiting for us to open the doors. But he wasn't.

We peered inside but it was too dark to see anything except the steps that went down into the basement.

We said Gary's name over and over.

But there was no answer.

That's when Jodi started to panic a bit, and Jodi NEVER panics.

So we all started shouting, "GARY! GARY! CAN YOU HEAR US?!"

But Gary didn't shout back.

We had NO IDEA what to do so that's when Jodi said, "The Den. Now!" and then she started to run, so we all followed her because The Den is our secret meeting place under the stairs that go up to the boys' toilets and

we ALWAYS meet there when we have to make SERIOUS PLANS.

But when we got there we all

GASPED.

Because Gary Petrie was sitting in The Den!

We stood there SHOCKED as Gary GRINNED at us and said, "It's about time!"

It took Jodi a minute to be able to speak, but then eventually she said, "How did YOU get here?!"

Gary laughed and said, "Why? Didn't think I'd make it out ALIVE, did you?!"

Then he stood up and put his ARMS in the air and yelled, "THE POWER OF THE RIVER GARRY RUNS THROUGH ME, REMEMBER? NOTHING CAN STOP ME!"

And Jodi hissed, "SHHHHHHHHH! You'll get us caught!"

But Gary DIDN'T "SHHHH". He just threw his head back and started LAUGHING a weird WILD laugh.

I shut the door and asked Gary if he was OK. Because he was acting even MORE annoying than usual.

But then the door

open again and I GASPED because I thought that we'd been CAUGHT by a TEACHER.

But it WASN'T a teacher. It was Maisie and she wasn't screaming any more. But she DID have about TWENTY bags of crisps and sweets in her arms!

Maisie RUSHED forward and dropped the crisps and sweets at Gary's feet and said, "There you go, Gary. I wasn't sure how much you'd need, so I just got you one of everything. I hope that's OK? Will it be enough?!"

Gary nodded loads and said thank you and then he started eating like he'd been starved for a WEEK.

That's when Jodi rolled her eyes and said

that it had only been ONE HOUR AND
TEN MINUTES that he'd been trapped
in the basement and that none of US had
eaten anything since then either.

But that's when Maisie turned to us and
her EYES were WIDE and she said, "Gary
has had a

TRAUMATIC EXPERIENCE.

He thought he would NEVER get out!"
And Gary nodded LOADS and opened
another bag of crisps and said, "My body
went into survival mode and started

EATING ITSELF."

So that's when we asked Gary how he'd managed to get out.

And that's when Maisie said, "Me."

We all turned our heads REALLY FAST and looked at her because we hadn't been expecting that!

Maisie told us that being stuck in a DARK BASEMENT is one of her TOP-THIRTY WORST FEARS and that that was why she had screamed. And that WHILE she was screaming she'd decided to KEEP screaming on PURPOSE so that she'd get sent to the nurse and be able to sneak away

to let Gary out.

We all STARED at Maisie because we were

 SHOCKED

that she'd made a

 SECRET PLAN

without us.

That's when Maisie said, "There's SOMETHING ELSE."

And then she took a deep breath and I saw

that her EYEBALLS were shaking a bit, so I knew that this was going to be BAD.

And then Maisie said, "Gary saw something."

And Jodi said, "What? What did he see?!"

Maisie looked at Gary, and Gary looked at Maisie, and then he opened his mouth and tried to speak but only CRISPS came out because his mouth was full.

That's when Gary started choking a bit and Jodi rolled her eyes and got behind him and said, "Gary, I'm about to perform the HEIMLICH MANOEUVRE on you." And then she squeezed him really sharply and

loads of CRISP CRUMBS came FLYING out of his mouth and all over the floor.

Maisie gave Gary a Ribena and he drank it ALL and then opened another bag of crisps, and Jodi rolled her eyes and said, "NO, GARY. No more crisps till you tell us what you saw."

And that's when Gary said, "You'd better sit down."

So we all sat down, but Jodi said that she would "PREFER TO STAND" and we all knew that she was doing it because she didn't like that Gary was trying to TAKE THE LEAD in the investigation and that this was her way of staying in CHARGE.

So that's when Gary stood up TOO and then he said, "I saw something. Well, I didn't actually SEE anything."

And Jodi put her hands on her hips and rolled her eyes.

"I mean, I HEARD something," said Gary. "It sounded like scraping or scratching."

And even though it was quite warm in The Den, I felt a SHIVER go down my back, because I did NOT like the idea of being locked in a DARK basement under the school with something that was making a

SCRAPING SOUND.

No one said anything for ages and then Jodi said, "Gary, I have to ask you this. Are

you telling us the truth?"

And I knew that Jodi was asking because sometimes Gary makes things UP. Like the time he told Miss Jones that it was his BIRTHDAY and she gave him a BISCUIT from her BISCUIT TIN and then later she told him off after she checked the SCHOOL COMPUTER and found out that it WASN'T his birthday AT ALL!

And that's when Gary put his hand on his chest and said, "I swear on the United States of America and the KING and on all these CRISPS that I heard weird SCRAPING and SCRATCHING noises."

That's when Jodi nodded, and I could tell that she believed him.

And then Jodi sat down on her upturned bucket and said, "OK, so now we know. There's SOMETHING DOWN THERE."

The Best Pizza in the WORLD

That night me and Zach waited outside our block of flats because Jodi's mum was picking us up.

When we got in the car Maisie was already there and she had a HUGE CAKE on her knee and she was smiling LOADS.

But Jodi WASN'T smiling.

Jodi's mum shouted hello at us because Jodi's mum shouts everything. My dad says that he thinks her EARS were DAMAGED by the HAIRDRYERS when she used to be hairdresser. But I think she's just a really LOUD person.

So anyway, me and Zach squeezed in next to Maisie and the

GIANT CAKE

and put our seat belts on.

Jodi's mum said, "Are you looking forward

to tonight?"

And Maisie screamed, "YES!"

And we all JUMPED and Jodi's mum started laughing.

But the REST of us didn't scream "YES" because we were

NOT excited.

Because we were on our way to

GARY PETRIE'S HOUSE.

When we got there Jodi's mum said,

"**WOW!** That's one cool house, isn't it?"

And we all

GASPED

because there was a **HOT TUB** in the **FRONT GARDEN** and it had

DISCO LIGHTS

above it.

Then, all of a sudden, **GARY** appeared,

and he was wearing a weird silk dressing gown thing over his clothes and he said, "WELCOME TO CASA GARY!"

Then he handed us all a glass of juice and said, "Gary's signature smoothie. I just made a fresh batch. It's mango, pineapple and guava. Enjoy!"

So we all took our drinks and Gary told us to follow him up the driveway and into his "CASA", and when we stepped inside we all

GASPED

because his house was HUGE inside and it

was actually just one big ROOM.

That's when Gary's DAD appeared and he was wearing an APRON that had flour all over it and I noticed that he even had some on his BALD HEAD, but I didn't say anything.

Then Gary's dad said, "WELCOME TO CASA PETRIE! Your pizzas will be ready in a MOMENTO!"

And I laughed a bit because I thought it was funny how much Gary's dad sounded like Gary when he said stuff and I realised that that must be why Gary says all the weird stuff that he does.

Then Gary said, "Thanks, Jeeves!"

And Gary's dad laughed and rubbed Gary's head, and Gary ducked and laughed and said, "Watch the hair, Dad!"

Gary's dad laughed some more and said, "You and that hair, boy! You were in the bathroom for over an hour messing with it!"

That's when I saw Gary's face go a bit red and I knew that it was because he was embarrassed that we knew he'd taken ages to do his hair all fancy because we were coming over and he was obviously trying to impress us.

Then Gary's dad asked us if we'd like the GRAND TOUR and we nodded. And that's when Gary's dad told us all about how downstairs used to be FOUR different rooms and that he'd knocked down all the walls and made it into ONE BIG ROOM with the kitchen and living room and dining room all in the same room.

Zach kept saying WOW and asking if he would be able to do that to his and his mum's

flat, but I couldn't concentrate because I was a bit worried that the TOILET was part of the BIG ROOM too and there was NO WAY I was using it if it was!

But then Gary's dad must have read my mind because he said, "Over there, lass."

And I looked and saw that there was a FAKE-DOOR thing that looked like a WALL unless you looked really closely. And then Gary's dad pressed it and it OPENED and Zach said, "NO WAY!"

That's when Gary said, "Dad designed it himself. He's maybe going to be on that *Grand Designs* programme. He's amazing!"

Gary's dad smiled and grabbed Gary by both cheeks and gave him a big KISS right on his forehead, and then they laughed and we all laughed too, because Gary's dad was really funny.

Then Gary's dad said, "Go and give your pals a tour of the rest of the house. I'll shout you down when your pizzas are ready!"

So we all went upstairs and Gary showed us the WHIRLPOOL BATH and WALK-IN RAIN SHOWER and HEATED TOILET SEAT.

Then Zach said he wanted to use the heated toilet seat so we all laughed and ran out and shut the door and left Zach inside.

Gary led us along the hall until we got to a door that said "THE PALACE" and Jodi said, "Let me guess. Your bedroom?"

Gary grinned and said, "Why, yes!" and then he pushed the door open and I was

because the first thing I saw was a FULL WALL OF BOOKS.

Maisie

and ran over and began touching all the SPINES of the books and saying, "Oh! I love this one! And can I borrow this one?!"

And Gary said, "What is mine is yours. Take as many as you like. I've read them all."

I looked at Jodi and she looked just as shocked as I did because I had

NO IDEA

Gary loved books and I definitely wasn't expecting him to have a WHOLE WALL of them.

Then Gary sat down in a big antique-looking chair and said, "TV ON," and then we all heard this BUZZING SOUND and we turned and saw a HUGE TV appearing out of the bottom of Gary's bed.

That's when Gary said that his dad knew the person who INVENTED TV BEDS and that he'd given one to his dad for FREE when he'd fixed his BOILER and that he'd given it to Gary.

That's when Zach appeared and he saw the TV BED and he said, "WOW," and me and Jodi burst out laughing because we couldn't stop thinking about him sitting on the HEATED TOILET SEAT.

When it was time for pizza, Gary's dad said we were having it in the garden and that's when we saw that he was actually COOKING it in the garden too and that he had this big pizza-oven thing with REAL FLAMES.

We all STARED at the pizza when it came out of the oven because we had

NO IDEA

what was on it.

Then Gary said, "The Gary Special! It's cheeseburgers and chips!"

We all stared at each and then I burst out

laughing because I'd never seen cheeseburger and chips on a pizza before!

Zach grabbed a piece and started MUNCHING, and then his EYES went WIDE.

I thought he'd burned his MOUTH because it had literally JUST come out of the oven! But then Zach said, "OH. MY. GOODNESS."

And then he completely DEMOLISHED

the rest of the slice and grabbed another.

So that's when we all took a slice (apart from Jodi who was waiting for the vegetarian one) and I was a bit surprised because Zach was RIGHT. It was DELICIOUS!

Gary stood up on his chair and clapped his hands and said, "BRAVO, FATHER! BRAVO!"

Then Gary's dad took a bow and then he brought ANOTHER pizza over and Gary said, "This is Dad's favourite pizza. Or, as we call it, The DADINATOR!"

We all looked and saw that it was COVERED in chilli peppers.

I wasn't brave enough to try it, but Jodi was because she LOVES really spicy things. But then she had to ask for a glass of MILK because the DADINATOR was far too spicy for her!

Gary's dad kept making different pizzas and letting us choose what to put on them and we were all having a GREAT TIME. And we were having such a great time that we totally forgot how ANNOYING Gary is and also that we'd come to his house to have a

SECRET MEETING

about the

SECRET BASEMENT

and the

SCRAPING SOUND

and to interview Gary's dad to try to find out

what he knew.

But then Gary said, "Dad, what happened

at school today with Mr Graves? What was

the emergency?"

And **THAT'S** when Gary's dad **STOPPED**

making pizza and got a WEIRD LOOK on his face.

Then he sat down next to us and said, "Aye, that was a strange one, that!"

And me and Jodi STARED at each other.

Then Gary's dad said, "He wanted me to move the old boiler in the basement. But he wouldn't tell me why. But I told him there's NO WAY that thing can be shifted – it weighs a ton! Looks like it's been there forever. Then, when I told him I could see something behind it, he asked me to leave and paid me for the job anyway, even though I didn't do anything! It was like he couldn't get me out of there fast enough!"

That's when Jodi put down her mushroom and chips pizza and said, "Mr Petrie, what did you see?"

And Gary's dad rubbed his bald head with both hands and said, "It was a bit weird, actually. There's no lighting down there, but when I flashed my torch behind the boiler I saw something

SHINING

back at me. And the second I mentioned it to Mr Graves he asked me to leave."

We watched as Gary's dad went back to singing and making the pizzas.

And then Gary whispered, "Whatever my dad found, Mr Graves obviously didn't want him to see it!"

And we knew that Gary was RIGHT.

We're On to You, Mr Graves!

The next day in school, Mr Graves looked like he'd been up all night again.

We watched from behind the big plant in reception while Mr Graves spoke to two of the DINNER LADIES.

That's when Gary said that we needed to

get CLOSER and that he had an IDEA, and then he started PUSHING the big plant CLOSER to Mr Graves really slowly until we were close enough to hear a bit better.

And **THAT'S** when we heard Mr Graves say, "You can't tell a **SOUL!**"

And then the dinner ladies put their **ICE-CREAM SCOOPS** against their chests and said, "Your secret's safe with us. We won't tell anyone about the treasure."

And we all

GASPED.

None of us could concentrate in class and we kept getting told off for **DRAMATIC WHISPERING**. And I knew that if we didn't

stop, we were going to get a DETENTION.
But we couldn't stop. Because this was

HUGE.

There was ⭐ ⭐ ⭐ — TREASURE — ⭐ ⭐ ⭐ ⭐ ⭐

in the SCHOOL BASEMENT.

Jodi kept shaking her head and saying that
what Mr Graves was doing was GREEDY

and probably **ILLEGAL**, because he was obviously trying to **FIND** and **KEEP** the treasure for himself.

Jodi's eyes were **WIDE** and they were sort of **SHINING** in a way I'd never seen before.

And then she started speaking **REALLY FAST** about how **WE** should be the ones to find the treasure and that we'd probably be **FAMOUS** and get **MEDALS** and that we could give loads to **CHARITY** and keep the rest to pay for a SCHOOL SWIMMING POOL.

Then Zach said that we should keep some for ourselves too, and Jodi smiled and said, "Maybe just ONE bar of gold each."

Maisie put a hand over her mouth and started giggling loads.

And none of us could believe it because we were probably going to be

MILLIONAIRES.

But then a chair scraped across the floor really loud and Gary Petrie jumped out of his

seat and started hopping from one leg to the other saying, "Miss! Miss! I need the toilet!"

And even though it was almost time for lunch, Miss Jones said OK and Gary rushed out (even though she **NEVER** normally lets us go right before lunch).

But that's when Jodi

GASPED

and said that she'd **SEEN** Gary go to the toilet at break and that he hadn't even had a **JUICE** and that he'd only had **CRISPS**.

Then Jodi put her hand up and asked if

SHE could go to the toilet too, but Miss Jones said no and that the bell for lunch was about to go any minute.

Jodi kept FIDGETING and saying that she didn't TRUST Gary and that she didn't think he needed the toilet and that he was just PRETENDING that he did so that he could get out of class.

We all STARED at each other because we had

what Jodi was going on about.

But then Jodi's eyes went wide and she came REALLY CLOSE to my face and said, "Don't you see what's happening?!"

But I just shook my head because all I could see were her HUGE EYEBALLS.

That's when Jodi said that Gary had OVERHEARD us talking about giving most of the treasure to CHARITY and that HE wanted to find it and keep it for HIMSELF so he could buy loads more fancy things like DISCO HOT TUBS and TV BEDS.

Maisie

GASPED

and said, "No! Gary wouldn't do that!"

And that's when Jodi said that he WOULD,

and that we couldn't trust ANYONE now that TREASURE was involved and that money

CHANGED PEOPLE.

She looked at her watch and said, "There's still FIVE FULL MINUTES before the bell goes. We can't wait that long. I need to do something."

Then, before anyone could stop her, Jodi got up and RAN out of the classroom.

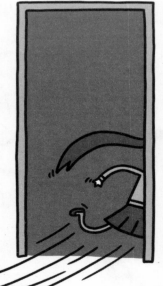

We all

and Miss Jones said, "JODI! Come back!"

But Jodi DIDN'T come back. And she didn't even close the door behind her.

That's when Zach stood up and said, "She can't go down there alone!"

And then ZACH ran out of the classroom too.

Miss Jones was shouting at Jodi and Zach to "COME BACK THIS INSTANT" and everyone was GASPING and asking Miss

Jones what was happening, and it was

CHAOS.

That's when Miss Jones told us all to STAY PUT and that she was going to fetch Mr Graves.

As soon as she left, I looked at Maisie.

And Maisie looked at me.

And then she nodded.

Then we ran too.

When we got
to the basement,
the doors were
open.

I peered inside but
I couldn't see anything.

I looked at Maisie and
her EYES had gone all
SWIRLY, so I knew that there
was NO WAY she was going inside.
THAT'S when we heard a SCREAM.

And I recognised the scream.

It was Jodi!

Race to Find the Treasure!

I turned and looked at Maisie but she'd **FAINTED**. So I quickly put her in the **RECOVERY POSITION** and took a **DEEP BREATH** and started walking down the steps into the **DARK BASEMENT**.

I couldn't see Jodi anywhere and I was

PANICKING because the last thing I'd heard was a SCREAM and now there was SILENCE.

Then suddenly I felt something touch my shoulder and I SCREAMED and spun round because I was

TERRIFIED

in case it was some sort of

BASEMENT GHOST,

but it was just JODI.

I checked that Jodi still had all her arms and legs, and then I gave her a big hug and said, "I heard you scream!"

But then something ELSE touched my OTHER shoulder and I SCREAMED AGAIN.

That's when Zach said, "Sorry! Sorry! Just me!"

I had to crouch down for a minute to CALM DOWN after all the SHOULDER SCARES and that's when Jodi told me that she was fine and that she'd screamed because she'd bumped into a SKELETON and I

GASPED

and said, "WHAT?!"

Zach laughed and shone his PHONE TORCH against the basement wall and said, "It's OK. It's fake! It's from that school play the old Year 6s did, remember?"

I nodded because I did remember, but it was still SUPER CREEPY being in a DARK BASEMENT with a SKELETON and loads of SHOULDER TOUCHING.

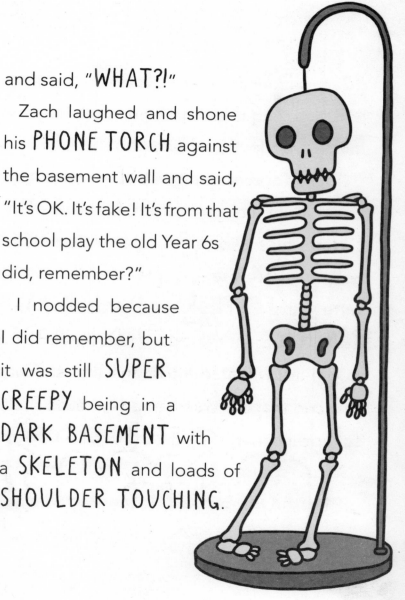

Zach shone his torch around the basement and said, "It's massive down here! I think it must go under the whole school!"

I looked around and saw that the basement was full of creepy school furniture from Olden Times, like school desks with the little holes for INK when people used to have to write with FEATHERS instead of PENS or PENCILS.

Jodi said that they hadn't found Gary yet, but that he was obviously down here somewhere looking for the BOILER that his dad had spotted something SHINY behind.

Then she whispered, "No more screaming,

OK? I don't want Gary to know that **WE** know he's down here. We need to find the treasure before he does. Or catch him trying to take it for himself!"

So I nodded, but I was a bit worried that I **WAS** going to scream again because there were **COBWEBS** and **FREAKY FURNITURE** and **SKELETONS** in the basement and, to be completely honest, I was starting to worry that there might be **MICE** too.

I knew that it was just as well that Maisie had fainted **UPSTAIRS** because she would have **DEFINITELY** fainted the second she

105

saw the skeleton.

Zach went in front because he had the torch, and I held on to the back of Zach's jumper and Jodi held on to mine and we crept through the dark basement.

Jodi tugged on my T-shirt and whispered, "Tell Zach to go left."

So I whispered to Zach to go left. But Zach ignored me and went RIGHT.

Then Jodi started getting ANNOYED and tugging on my jumper LOADS, saying, "Left! Tell him LEFT!"

But then Zach stopped and said, "GOTCHA!" and we looked and saw that Zach was shining his phone torch on something.

That's when Zach said, "I think that's the boiler."

So we rushed over and Zach shone his

torch behind the boiler, but we couldn't see anything shiny.

Jodi said that we needed to get BEHIND the boiler ourselves, but the gap wasn't big enough to fit through and there was NO WAY we could move the old boiler because it was MASSIVE.

Zach got down on his hands and knees and pushed his arm through as far as he could and shone his phone torch around.

Then, all of a sudden, Zach GASPED, and Jodi hissed, "What? What is it?!"

That's when Zach looked up at us and he had TEARS in his eyes.

That's when I thought that he'd found GOLD and that we were about to become

INSTANT MILLIONAIRES,

and I grabbed Jodi's hand and squeezed it, and she squeezed back and GRINNED at me.

We both stood there smiling and waiting to hear how many BARS OF GOLD Zach had found.

But Zach wasn't smiling.

And that's when he pulled his arm out from behind the boiler.

And then he said, "I dropped my phone."

I looked at Jodi, and she looked at me, but before either of us could say anything we spotted TORCHLIGHT in the distance, and Jodi hissed, "That must be Gary. Hide! Under the stairs!"

So we rushed back over to the staircase and hid behind it.

We watched as the torch got closer and CLOSER.

But then, all of a sudden, we heard FOOTSTEPS on the stairs, and I GASPED and Jodi covered my mouth with her hand.

But then I recognised the SHOES. So I

pulled Jodi's hand away and whispered, "It's Maisie!"

That's when Jodi LEAPED out and GRABBED Maisie and put her hand over HER mouth and pulled her under the staircase. And she did it all in ONE MOVE.

Maisie's EYES looked PANICKED, so I patted her knee and put my finger up to my lips to show Maisie that we had to be SILENT, and Maisie nodded nervously and Jodi took her hand off her mouth.

Then Zach pointed to the torchlight in the distance and whispered, "It's Gary. He's trying to steal all the treasure for himself. We're going to catch him and stop him."

But Maisie just STARED at us.

Then she shook her head REALLY SLOWLY and said, "No, it's not."

We all turned and STARED at Maisie.

And then she said, "Gary's up there! I just

saw him coming out of the toilet!"

We all watched Maisie's shaking finger point above our heads at the ceiling.

And Jodi said, "What?!"

And Maisie nodded.

Then Zach did a GULP and said, "If Gary's up there … then who's THAT over there?"

And THAT'S when the torch went out and we all

SCREAMED.

Sent to the Head Teacher's Office

We were all sitting on the seats outside the head teacher's office.

Jodi said that it must have been Mr Graves in the basement searching for the TREASURE. And that he'd seen us run out and that now we were all about to get EXPELLED.

Then, all of a sudden, GARY turned up and sat down next to us.

We asked him why he was here because HE hadn't run out of class without permission OR been caught in the basement by Mr Graves like we had.

But Gary wouldn't talk to ANY of us. Not even Maisie. Because he knew that we thought he'd gone to steal the TREASURE without us because Maisie had told him when we got back to class when he'd asked us where we'd been.

Then one of the office ladies stuck her

head out of the little glass window and said, "Mr Graves will see you now. In you go."

So I looked at Jodi and she looked at Zach and Zach looked at Maisie, because none of us wanted to be the first one to walk in. But then Gary got up and walked in first and we followed.

We all stood in a line in front of Mr Graves's desk and waited for him to look up from whatever he was reading. And that's when I noticed that he had SCRATCHES all over his hands and I knew that they were probably from searching for TREASURE in the basement.

That's when Gary said, "What are you reading, Mr Graves?"

And we all STARED at Gary because we couldn't believe that Gary was trying to have a CHAT with Mr Graves when he'd been sent to his office.

Mr Graves looked up, but he didn't say anything, and that's when I noticed that his EYES looked all weird and BLOODSHOT, and I knew that it was because he was probably EXHAUSTED and worried because he hadn't found the TREASURE yet.

That's when Mr Graves folded up whatever

he had been reading and said, "How can I help you all?"

And we all looked at each other because HE had been the one who had asked to see us.

Then he said, "Miss Jones said I needed to speak to you?! What is it about?"

That's when Gary said, "It's all my fault, Mr Graves. Everyone ran out of class because they were worried about me because I said that I thought I was going to projectile vomit because I thought my cereal might have been off. They were just worried about me. It wasn't their fault."

We all stood in

SHOCK

because Gary was actually trying to HELP US, even though he'd just found out that we'd ACCUSED HIM of being a TRAITOR.

Mr Graves looked at us all and then said, "That's a good friend you've got there. It's good to have a best friend. Someone who you can always turn to ... someone who's always there when you get home after a long day..."

Then Mr Graves got all TEARY-EYED and

he got up and went into his little bathroom and shut the door.

We all stood there and didn't move because we didn't know what do. And then we heard Mr Graves **BLOWING HIS NOSE** and Zach whispered, "Yuck!"

Then I whispered, "What's going on?!"

And that's when Jodi said that she thought Mr Graves

was CRACKING under the pressure of trying to find the treasure before anyone else did.

Jodi leaned over and unfolded the thing Mr Graves had been reading and I could feel my heart POUNDING in my chest because Mr Graves was RIGHT THERE in his little bathroom and I knew that he could open the door at ANY SECOND and that Jodi would get caught SNOOPING.

That's when Jodi said, "It's BOILER instructions! He's probably trying to figure out how to get behind it!"

Then suddenly we heard a PHONE RING and we all JUMPED, and Jodi quickly folded

the paper back up the way it had been and stood up straight JUST as Mr Graves came RUSHING out of his little toilet and picked his mobile phone up off his desk and said, "HELLO?! HELLO?!"

I could feel an ACTUAL BEAD OF SWEAT starting to run down my face because of the PRESSURE.

I had

what was about to happen next, but that's when Mr Graves waved at us to leave. And

we were

SHOCKED.

Because we thought we were going to get in **BIG TROUBLE** for being in the basement. But we didn't!

Mr Graves took his mobile phone into the toilet and **CLOSED THE DOOR**.

So we started to leave but when we were nearly out, Jodi stopped and said, "Wait," and then she tiptoed back and put her **EAR** against the toilet door.

I held my **BREATH** because I was

TERRIFIED that Mr Graves would open the door and that Jodi would fall into the little bathroom and get EXPELLED FOR LIFE for SPYING.

We watched as Jodi listened for a bit and then suddenly her EYES went WIDE.

And then she ran RIGHT PAST US and said, "DEN!"

So we ran.

Cheese and Onion

When we got to The Den, Jodi told us that she'd heard Mr Graves say "LOST TREASURE" and "IT'S A RACE AGAINST TIME".

So we knew that Mr Graves hadn't managed to find the LOST TREASURE yet either.

Then Jodi said, "That means there's still time for US to find it first!"

We all agreed that the SHINY THING behind the boiler must be the treasure and that we should focus our search there.

Zach agreed LOADS and said that we needed to find a way to get behind the boiler ASAP, and also that if he went home without his PHONE his mum would GROUND HIM FOR LIFE.

Jodi started pacing backwards and forwards and saying, "We need a plan. We need a plan!"

That's when Gary said, "I have a plan."

Jodi stopped and spun round and said, "What plan?!"

But then Gary just crossed his arms and said, "WELL, maybe you'll just have to trust me FOR ONCE, Jodi." And then he got up and walked BACKWARDS all the way to the door and he pointed at each of us for AGES until he got there.

Then he said, "Meet me at the basement doors after school dinners. BE THERE!" And then he ran away.

Zach said, "What was THAT?"

Jodi just shook her head and said, "THAT was NOTHING. He doesn't have a plan."

But I didn't say anything. Because I wasn't so sure.

As soon as we finished dinners, Maisie said that we should go and meet Gary at the basement doors and me and Zach agreed.

But Jodi said that she wasn't going and that it was POINTLESS and that Gary just wanted to be in CHARGE of the investigation and that he would SAY ANYTHING to gain CONTROL because he was

OBSESSED with BEING IN CHARGE.

I just LOOKED at Jodi when she said that and Jodi said, "What? What are you looking at me like that for, Izzy?!"

But I didn't say anything.

And then Jodi said, "What are you trying to say?"

And I STILL didn't say anything.

Then Jodi said, "I'M not like that if THAT'S what you mean!"

And she looked at Zach, but he just did an awkward WHISTLING THING and looked up at the roof, even though there wasn't anything to see up there.

Then Jodi looked at Maisie and said, "I'm not like that. Am I, Maisie?"

But Maisie just looked down at her shoes and didn't say anything.

Because Jodi **WAS** like that.

Jodi didn't say anything for ages and then eventually she said, "Fine. Let's go."

So we all sneaked over to the

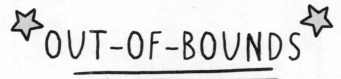

OUT-OF-BOUNDS

bit of the playground, and we kept our

BACKS TO THE WALL AT ALL TIMES, just like Jodi had trained us to, so we'd be harder to spot.

Then Jodi said, "Look. He's not there. I knew it."

But then, all of a sudden, Gary came RUSHING towards us from the other direction and his face was BRIGHT RED.

Gary was TOTALLY out of breath and he could hardly speak.

Maisie made Gary sit down on the ground and do the BREATHING EXERCISES that she needs to do to make sure she doesn't faint all the time and that's when I saw Gary's bag MOVE.

I GASPED and pointed at Gary's bag and said, "Something just moved in there!"

Gary tried to talk but he was still really out of breath, and it was obvious that he'd been running for AGES.

I STARED at Gary as he put his backpack on his knee and said, "This … is … plan." And then he unzipped the bag a tiny bit and a PAW came out and started waving all over the place.

We all

GASPED

and took a step back.

And Gary said, "Cheese. Onion."

We were totally confused because Gary was being REALLY WEIRD and he'd brought some sort of WILD ANIMAL to school.

But then a CAT popped its head out of the gap, and Gary grinned and said, "Meet Cheese and Onion. SHE'S the plan!"

Cat Cam CHAOS

Jodi looked  SHOCKED,

but then Gary said, "Go! Before someone sees!"

So we all rushed over to the basement with Gary and the CAT in the BAG, even though we had

what the plan actually was.

Gary started to open the doors to the basement but then Maisie said, "Wait! What if Mr Graves or maybe SOMEONE ELSE is down there hunting for the missing treasure? We'll get caught and expelled!"

Maisie's LEGS started to SHAKE VIOLENTLY, so me and Zach held one of

her arms each just in case she SUDDENLY DROPPED.

But then Gary smiled and said, "Don't worry, Maisie. We WON'T get caught. I have a PLAN."

Jodi made a loud BREATHING SOUND out of her NOSTRILS, and I knew that she did that because Gary STILL wasn't sharing

THE PLAN

with us.

That's when Gary put his hand in the bag and pulled out something that WASN'T a

cat and said,

"TA-DA!"

We all looked at what Gary had in his hand, but we didn't say anything because we didn't know what it was.

Then Zach said, "Is that a head torch?!"

And that's when Gary said, "Oh no, Zachary. It's MUCH more than that! It's my own INVENTION."

And then he put the CAT BACKPACK

on his back and said, "Follow me and be AMAAAAAAAZED at my brilliance!"

So we followed Gary down into the basement and watched as he unzipped his bag and a HUGE ginger cat jumped out!

"BEHOLD Cheese and Onion!" said Gary. "The

NINJA CAT.

I've been training her for years."

Cheese and Onion lay down on the

basement floor and yawned.

Then Gary said, "Don't let her FOOL YOU. She's always on HIGH ALERT. Ready for action!"

We watched as Cheese and Onion rolled on to her back and stretched her legs and CAT TOES.

Zach laughed and said that she looked a bit like she was about to fall asleep.

But Gary shook his head and said, "That's just what she WANTS you to think. ALWAYS the

MASTER OF DISGUISE."

Then he said that Cheese and Onion was actually WARMING UP and doing all her CAT STRETCHES so that she could POUNCE at a split second's notice.

But then Cheese and Onion's tummy made a weird noise and we all smelled a REALLY BAD SMELL and Jodi covered her noise and said, "Yuck. Was that her?"

And we all laughed.

But then Gary said, "BEHOLD, MERE EARTHLINGS! My most recent INVENTION."

And then he held up the head-torch-helmet thing. "Allow me to introduce to you the Petrie Cat Cam DELUXE!"

Then Gary bent down and put the little helmet on Cheese and Onion's head and fastened it under her chin and her tummy made another noise and we all covered our noses just in case.

That's when Gary told us that he'd ADAPTED a normal head torch so that it could fit a CAT and that he'd added a MINI CAMERA that he took off his dad's mountain bike.

That's when Jodi said, "WOW." And I could tell that she meant it and that she was IMPRESSED.

Gary smiled LOADS and said, "Look! Look!"

And then he switched it on and the little torch came on and Cheese and Onion started chasing the light from her own head torch all over the place. Gary laughed and

said, "See! She's ready for action!"

Zach asked if he could stroke her, because Zach LOVES cats, but Gary said no and that Cheese and Onion was

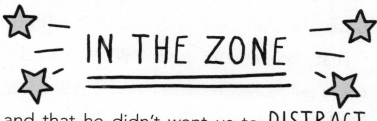

IN THE ZONE

and that he didn't want us to DISTRACT her.

That's when he told us that he'd run home at lunchtime to make the CAT CAM and that he'd also shown Cheese and Onion photos of TREASURE on his computer. And that she'd seen at least FIFTY pictures

of treasure and that she had even MEOWED to see MORE.

Jodi's eyes went wide, and she said, "Wait. You made the CAT CAM at lunch?!"

Gary nodded and said, "I make stuff like that all the time. It's easy when you're me." And then he winked at us.

I looked at Jodi and I could tell that she was even MORE impressed, and also that she was probably thinking about all the

SECRET-MISSION STUFF

she was going to ask Gary to make for us.

I said that I was a bit worried about letting Gary's cat LOOSE in the huge basement in case she got LOST but that's when Gary said, "Never fear! She's well trained. Cheese and Onion has been waiting for a mission like this her whole life!"

Then Gary said, "Cheese-Cheese! UP!"

And Cheese and Onion LEAPED from the ground all the way up on to Gary's SHOULDERS and then sat there PURRING loudly, and Gary grinned and patted her head through the CAT CAM.

We all GASPED and Maisie clapped her hands because we'd never seen a cat do a

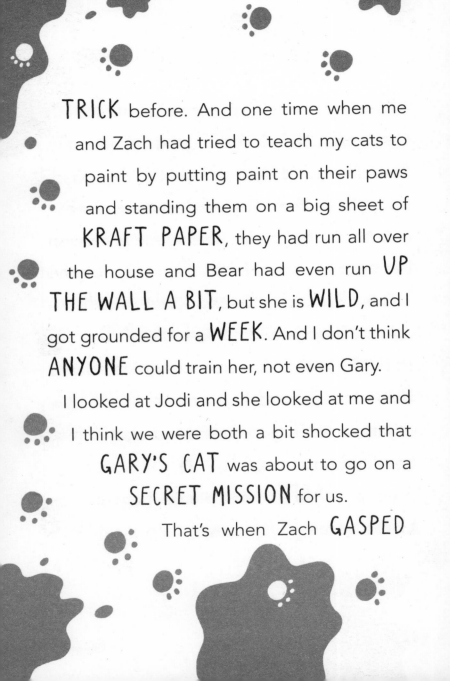

TRICK before. And one time when me and Zach had tried to teach my cats to paint by putting paint on their paws and standing them on a big sheet of KRAFT PAPER, they had run all over the house and Bear had even run UP THE WALL A BIT, but she is WILD, and I got grounded for a WEEK. And I don't think ANYONE could train her, not even Gary.

I looked at Jodi and she looked at me and I think we were both a bit shocked that GARY'S CAT was about to go on a SECRET MISSION for us.

That's when Zach GASPED

and said, "She'll fit behind the boiler!"

And Gary nodded and said, "Exactamundo!"

Gary picked up the cat and put her down next to the old boiler. And then he showed her a photo of TREASURE on his phone and we all watched as she STARED at it.

Then Gary patted her little head and said, "FIND," and the cat disappeared behind the boiler.

We all RAN back over to our hiding spot under the stairs and Gary took out his phone and said, "Are you ready for Gary's amazing CAT CAM?"

And we all nodded, so Gary pressed a button on his phone and that's when we were able to see what CHEESE AND ONION could see.

We all STARED at the screen as Cheese and Onion walked about behind the boiler.

At first it was a bit shaky, but then, once we got used to it, it was like BEING Cheese and Onion. And THAT'S when we saw that there was a little DOORWAY behind the boiler!

Jodi

and said, "That must be where the treasure is! It's a SECRET ROOM!"

Gary put the phone screen close to his mouth and said, "Go, Cheese! DOOR. Go!"

And then he looked at us and said, "Two-way microphone so she can hear me." And he waggled his eyebrows for a bit.

We all watched as Cheese and Onion stopped at the doorway.

And Gary said, "Go, Cheese. Go, Cheesy-weesy. Gary-wary give you big cat cuddly-wuddly if you do!"

We all STARED at Gary.

And then he looked up at us and said, "What? That's just how she likes me to talk to her, OK? No big deal."

Jodi smirked and said, "Oh no. No big deal at ALL ... Gary-wary."

Gary ignored her and kept talking to Cheese and Onion. But she wouldn't budge. She just seemed to be sitting there

STARING, because all we could see was the doorway.

That's when Zach said that he thought she'd seen something through the doorway with her

and that it might be all the piles of SHINY TREASURE and that she was probably STUNNED by how AMAZING it looked.

But then Cheese and Onion started to make a

WEIRD SOUND.

And Gary said, "Uh-oh."

And I knew why he'd said it because that's the sound MY cats make when they're scared.

We watched as Cheese and Onion started BACKING AWAY from the door, making the weird low sound, and then, all of a sudden, she went

WILD

and started SCREECHING and the camera was going ALL OVER THE PLACE.

We all

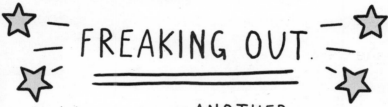

GASPED

because Cheese and Onion was

FREAKING OUT.

And then we heard **ANOTHER** sound. A

WAILING SOUND.

That's when Gary said, "That's not Cheese and Onion!"

And then we heard more SCREECHING, and it was SO LOUD that we had to COVER OUR EARS.

Maisie fainted on to my lap and Gary screamed, "CHEESE-CHEESE! COME! COME!" into the phone.

Then, all of a sudden, the SCREECHING and WAILING stopped and we saw Cheese and Onion come RACING towards us and I thought she was going to jump up on to Gary's shoulders but she didn't. She RAN right up the stairs and out of the basement.

I thought Gary would run after her. But he didn't. He just sat there not moving.

I thought that he was probably in

until I noticed that he was staring at his phone.

And he said, "The CAT CAM fell off..."

And that's when we all looked at the screen and saw that the CAT CAM was on the ground pointing towards the little doorway into the room behind the boiler.

Jodi gasped and said, "I see shining! Look!

It's the treasure!"

But then Gary shook his head really slowly and ZOOMED in.

And that's when we saw it.

We saw what was shining.

And it WASN'T treasure.

We all

GASPED

and Gary said, "We need to get out of here."

And he was RIGHT.

Shining Eyes

It took us AGES to find Cheese and Onion, and when we eventually did she was curled up SHAKING behind the old bike shed.

Gary put her inside his jumper, and me and Zach carried Maisie by a leg and an arm each and we RAN all the way to The Den.

Once we were inside, Gary checked that Cheese and Onion was OK and that she wasn't hurt. Then Jodi said that Cheese and Onion had had a

TRAUMATIC EXPERIENCE

and that she was obviously in

SHOCK

and SHAKING and that we needed to STABILISE HER TEMPERATURE so that her internal organs didn't FAIL.

Jodi said that we needed to lie Cheese and Onion and Maisie TOGETHER under a blanket so that they could share BODY HEAT. So we did that and as SOON as we did Cheese and Onion started PURRING.

Then Jodi suddenly sat down on the FLOOR and Jodi only EVER sits on the floor when she says she feels DIZZY, so I knew that Jodi was probably a bit in shock herself.

I sat down on the floor with Jodi so she wasn't on her own and she did a little smile at me.

Then Gary said, "Those loud weird noises didn't come from Cheese and Onion. I've never heard anything like that before!"

I nodded loads because I have two cats and I have never heard anything like that before either.

That's when Zach took a deep breath and

he took ages to let it out. And then he said,
"It didn't sound right. It sounded

OTHER-WORLDLY."

Then Jodi took a DEEP BREATH and
said, "But we have to talk about what we
SAW. That shining wasn't treasure."

No one said ANYTHING for ages after
Jodi said that, and I think that it was because
we were ALL in a bit of shock, actually.

We sat in silence staring at each other
because we were obviously ALL thinking
the same thing but no one wanted to be the

one to say it.

Because if you say it, it makes it feel more REAL. And more TERRIFYING.

And that's when Maisie's little quivery voice said, "It was EYES! The shining was EYES."

And we all looked at her because we knew there was more, but that Maisie needed a moment.

Then she gulped and said,

"THERE'S A BEAST IN THE BASEMENT!"

There's a Beast in the Basement!

When we got back to class, Jodi asked Miss Jones if Gary could sit at OUR table during PROJECT TIME and Miss Jones looked a bit SHOCKED. And then she said, "Erm ... yes?"

I knew that Miss Jones was shocked

because it's pretty obvious that Jodi and Gary don't usually get along. And they never have since Year One when Jodi wouldn't let Gary Petrie borrow her **GOOD PENS** so he **LICKED** her pencil case (which is disgusting because sometimes Gary is disgusting).

So anyway, Gary came and sat at our table and he looked **REALLY HAPPY** about it, and **THAT'S** when Jodi said that the secret meeting had **OFFICIALLY BEGUN** and that we needed to talk about **THE BEAST**. I couldn't believe that this was happening and that we were sitting there talking about how there was an **ACTUAL WILD BEAST**

in the SCHOOL BASEMENT.

Jodi said that we needed to figure out what it was and what it wanted.

And that's when Maisie said, "No, no, no, no!" And she started shaking her head SO VIOLENTLY that the ends of her pigtails were actually hitting me and Zach in the face.

Maisie said that we needed to forget ALL ABOUT the BEAST and pretend that we'd never seen it and never go down into the basement EVER AGAIN.

So that's when I said, "But what about Mr Graves? He doesn't KNOW about the beast. He might get hurt if we don't do something."

And then Zach said, "And what about my PHONE?!"

Jodi nodded and said that doing nothing WASN'T AN OPTION.

Then Gary looked around to make sure Miss Jones wasn't close by and then he took a deep breath and whispered, "I think I know what's happening."

And we all leaned forward and he said, "I think the beast might be GUARDING the treasure!"

And we all

GASPED.

That's when Gary said that he'd read all these BOOKS about BEASTS and how in one of them a BEAST had been CURSED and forced to guard a king's TREASURE for ONE THOUSAND YEARS.

That's when Maisie's EYES went wide and

she said, "Oh! Wait! I've read that one too! The beast had **THREE HEADS** and would **ATTACK** anyone who tried to steal the treasure!"

And **THAT'S** when I remembered the **SCRATCHES** that I'd seen on Mr Graves's **HANDS** when we were in his office.

And I **GASPED** and said, "I think Mr Graves **KNOWS** about the beast! That's why he looked so **SCARED** all the time and why he was **CRYING** during assembly!"

Jodi **GASPED BACK** at me and said, "The **SCRATCHES** on his hands!"

And I nodded loads.

That's when Jodi said that Mr Graves had obviously already come FACE TO FACE with the beast, or at least HAND TO CLAW with it.

"I can't believe this!" said Maisie. "Why would Mr Graves keep trying to find the TREASURE once he'd discovered that there was a BEAST guarding it! It's so dangerous!"

But then Zach said that maybe Mr Graves was having MONEY TROUBLES and that he needed money SO BADLY that he was willing to face a BEAST to get it.

And THAT'S when I remembered about

the LETTER we took home last month that said the SCHOOL BUS was OUT OF ORDER and that there weren't enough SCHOOL FUNDS to fix it. And that THAT meant school trips and going SWIMMING were

CANCELLED UNTIL FURTHER NOTICE.

Gary gasped and said, "That's why there's no little tomato ketchup packets at dinners any more! Our school's got no money!"

Then Maisie said that that explained the
HOLEY CURTAINS in our classroom too.
And the broken toilet seats in the girls'
toilets.

And Gary said that the dinner ladies were
DEFINITELY giving out at least

THREE FEWER CHIPS

at dinners than they used to and that soon
we'd probably all only get

ONE CHIP EACH.

Jodi nodded LOADS and said that it also explained Mr Graves's BATTERED SHOES and how he kept wearing the same OLD JUMPER to school every day, even though it was covered in HORRIBLE BOBBLY BITS.

Then Jodi said, "He's probably got NO money left at all because he's spent all his OWN money trying to fix everything that's broken at school!"

That's when we all felt really GRATEFUL for Mr Graves because we knew that he was a good head teacher because he was willing to face a BEAST so that we could

get **TOMATO KETCHUP** at school dinners again.

And then, all of a sudden, I heard

WAILING.

At first I thought that I was **IMAGINING** it because I was **TERRIFIED** that there was a **BEAST** with **THREE HEADS** in the **SCHOOL BASEMENT**. But Jodi had heard it **TOO**.

She got down on the ground and put her ear against the wall and then she said, "It's coming from the basement."

And we saw that there was a VENT.

Then, before we could say ANYTHING ELSE, there was a high-pitched

SCREECHING SOUND

and the whole CLASS heard it.

Miss Jones looked a bit shocked and then she opened the window and said, "Calm down, everyone. It's OK. It's just the seagulls!"

But we knew that it WASN'T the seagulls.

Maisie gasped and said, "Mr Graves must be down there now. What if he's somehow managed to get behind the boiler and the beast has GOT HIM?!"

That's when Gary stood up and put BOTH FISTS in the air and said, "We have to help Mr Graves DEFEAT THE BEAST."

And Miss Jones said, "Sit down, Gary!"

Then Jodi stood up and put her HAND out in front of her and said, "Yes! Are you all in?"

And Miss Jones said, "What's going on over there?!"

I looked at Zach and Zach looked at Maisie and Maisie looked at Gary. And then we all took a deep breath and put our hands on top of Jodi's one by one.

And then Jodi said, "Team Take Down the Beast! Let's do this!"

And then, before Miss Jones could stop us, we ran out of class. Again!

It's All Going to be OK, Mr Graves!

When we got to the basement the doors were already open, so we knew that Mr Graves was DOWN THERE and that he'd WOKEN THE BEAST because we'd heard the SCREECHING.

Gary went into his bag and took out two

torches and gave one to Jodi and kept one for himself.

Then Zach said, "How are we going to do this?! We don't have nets or a cage or tranquilliser darts or ANYTHING like that."

That's when Gary and Maisie LOOKED at each other and said,

"WE KNOW"

at the EXACT same time.

Then Gary looked at Maisie, and Maisie nodded and said, "We're going to solve the riddle."

I was TOTALLY confused and thought that Maisie needed a little lie-down because of all the

TRAUMA and STRESS.

But then Gary said, "She's right. Beasts who are guarding something always have a RIDDLE that needs solving and it's the only way to defeat a GUARDING BEAST."

I looked at Maisie and saw that she was actually SMILING.

And then she said, "I'm really good at riddles. I love them!"

I looked at Jodi and she nodded, so that's when we went down the stairs into the basement. But I wasn't feeling very good about it. Because I would have **MUCH** rather had a **CAGE** or a **TRANQUILISER** than a **RIDDLE**.

When we got to the bottom of the stairs Maisie didn't seem scared at **ALL** and said, "The riddle will be written on something close to the beast's lair. It's probably on the boiler. Let's go." And then Maisie actually

LED THE WAY.

Jodi raised her eyebrows and looked at me, and I did the same back because I was just as surprised as Jodi that Maisie was being so CONFIDENT and IN CHARGE. And that made me feel a LOT better about the whole RIDDLE THING because she obviously knew what she was talking about.

When we got to the boiler, Jodi said that we

NEEDED TO
PREPARE OURSELVES

in case the beast had TAKEN Mr Graves into its LAIR, and that we'd be SAFE as long as we didn't try to put our HANDS or ARMS behind the old boiler to reach the treasure like Mr Graves had obviously done.

We all nodded and followed Jodi, and Zach gripped my hand and SQUEEZED it tight and said, "Do you think my phone's OK?"

But then before I could answer Maisie said, "There!"

And we saw that she was shining a torch on the side of the boiler and that there was something written on it.

"It says, 'Please leave closed after use'," said Maisie.

And then Gary said, "Oh! I know! It's DOOR. It's a riddle for the word 'DOOR'."

I thought that it was probably just some old BOILER INSTRUCTIONS, but Gary got down on his hands and knees and whispered, "Door!" through the gap at the back of the boiler.

But nothing happened.

Then Maisie shone the torch on something else and it wasn't an instruction – it looked like a POSTER had been glued to the boiler and it said:

LEAVE
WELL ALONE.

DISTURB
AT YOUR
OWN PERIL.

And Maisie GASPED and said, "This is definitely it. It means the treasure! The riddle is about the treasure!"

So Gary said "TREASURE" into the gap behind the boiler. But nothing happened.

So we told him to say it a bit LOUDER, so he did and that's when the

WAILING

started again.

I could feel my FEET going all HEAVY like they do when you're in an

EMERGENCY SITUATION.

And Jodi says that it's NATURAL and that it's called the FIGHT-OR-FLIGHT response, which means that your feet are trying to decide if they want to stay or if they want to run away. And I wasn't sure WHAT mine wanted to do because I was TERRIFIED.

That's when the WAILING started to get LOUDER, and Gary said, "Um ... I don't think that was the right word."

Then, all of a sudden, we heard FOOTSTEPS coming down the stairs, so we hid behind some boxes. And THAT'S when we saw Mr Graves and he got down on his

hands and knees next to the gap behind the boiler and whispered, "Treasure! Treasure!"

And that's when the WAILING got even LOUDER!

We watched as Mr Graves pulled up his old jumper and began to put his ARM into the gap and that's when I jumped out from behind the boxes and yelled,

"STOP! DON'T DO IT! WE DON'T NEED THE KETCHUP THAT MUCH!"

Mr Graves SCREAMED and fell backwards on to his bottom. But at least his arm was safe.

Mr Graves looked completely

to see me. And then when Jodi and the others stepped out from behind the boxes he stopped looking shocked and started to look a bit annoyed. And he said, "You shouldn't be down here! It's not safe!"

And Jodi said, "We know, Mr Graves. That's why we're here."

Mr Graves looked a bit confused and I knew that it was because **HE** didn't know that **WE** knew about the **LOST TREASURE** and

the BEAST that GUARDED IT.

Then Gary said, "There's no point shouting 'TREASURE' into the gap. That won't work."

And that's when Mr Graves's face went from SHOCK back to NORMAL and then to SADNESS. And then he said, "So you know."

And we said yes and that we'd come down because we were worried about him and wanted to help.

Mr Graves looked at us and smiled a little bit and said, "Thank you. But you really shouldn't be down here. It isn't safe."

Then, all of a sudden, we heard MORE footsteps coming down the stairs. LOADS of them! And we all GASPED (even Mr Graves) because it sounded like an ARMY was marching down the stairs.

And when we saw who it was Zach did a GULP and said, "Oh no. It's THEM."

Because it was the DINNER LADIES and they were marching towards us!

Gary started whispering something to Maisie about how the dinner ladies probably WORKED for THE BEAST and that somehow we'd just accidentally SUMMONED THEM.

And I looked at Maisie and saw that her EYES were starting to go all SWIRLY.

Then one of the dinner ladies shouted, "Mr Graves! Mr Graves! We've found your TREASURE!"

We all STARED at each other and Mr Graves leaped up.

The dinner ladies rushed over and then they all started moving out of the way so one of them could get through.

And when that dinner lady had reached the front she held something up in her arms and said, "Here's your lost treasure! We heard noises in the kitchen cupboard just now. And

when we opened the door we found THIS!"

We all looked at what the dinner lady was holding.

And that's when Mr Graves said, "That's not TREASURE!"

And it DEFINITELY WASN'T. Because it was

CHEESE AND ONION!

Then Gary said, "That's my cat! She must have escaped!"

We had

why the dinner ladies would think the lost treasure was a CAT.

But then Mr Graves SIGHED and said, "Treasure isn't ginger. She's black and white. And she isn't fat either."

And Gary said, "Hey! Cheese and Onion isn't FAT. She's a NINJA CAT." Then he said, "Cheese-Cheese! Come!"

And Cheese and Onion LEAPED out
of the dinner lady's arms and on to Gary's
shoulder.

Mr Graves STARED at Gary and Cheese
and Onion for AGES.

That's when Jodi said, "Mr Graves, what did
you mean when you said the TREASURE
was black and white?"

And then Zach said, "Yeah. I thought all
treasure was gold. Or maybe green if it's
CASH."

Mr Graves looked even MORE confused
than US! But he still didn't say anything. He
just sat there on the ground, STARING at

Gary and Cheese and Onion.

Then eventually he said, "Gary, did you train your cat to jump on your shoulder?"

And Gary nodded.

Then Mr Graves said, "Do you think you could train another cat to do something?"

So Gary nodded again and said that he could and that he'd trained his neighbour's cat to only poo in its OWN garden and not in his. And that he was thinking of starting a business called GARY PETRIE: CAT WHISPERER because he was so good with cats.

Mr Graves jumped to his feet and said,

"OK. Can I be your first customer then? I need your help."

We all watched as Mr Graves got back down on the ground and peeked into the gap behind the boiler and said, "I've been trying to get her to come out but it's not working. She won't come out. And when she gets close, I try to grab her, but she keeps SCRATCHING me. I think it's because she's scared."

We all STARED at each other.

And then Jodi said, "WHO won't come out? The BEAST?!"

Mr Graves laughed out loud and said, "Oh! I think you're the first person to make me laugh this week, Jodi! Thank you!"

And then he said, "She's mighty loud for a cat, isn't she? Maybe I'll nickname her **THE BEAST** from now on. That is, if Gary can help me get her out. She's been hiding in there all week!"

I spun my head round and looked at Jodi, and her mouth was hanging **WIDE OPEN.**

And that's when we all said,

"A CAT?!"

Then Zach said, "What about the lost

TREASURE?!"

And Mr Graves said, "That's my cat's name. Treasure's been lost for almost a **WEEK** now. I've been going out of my **MIND** with worry!"

We couldn't **BELIEVE** what we were hearing!

And then eventually I said, "We thought you were looking for lost treasure, Mr Graves!"

And Mr Graves said, "You what?!"

So that's when we explained about seeing

him searching in all the classroom cupboards and crawling along the corridor and crying in assembly and sneaking down into the basement and overhearing him say he needed to find LOST TREASURE when he was on his phone in the little bathroom in his office and how we'd seen the SCRATCHES on his HANDS. And how WE'D thought that he had been trying to

FACE THE BEAST

who guarded the lost treasure behind the boiler so that we could get a school bus that actually **WORKS** and get our **KETCHUP** back and not have to only have **ONE** chip with our fish fingers.

That's when Mr Graves and all the dinner ladies **STARED** at each other with their mouths **WIDE OPEN**. And then they all

BURST OUT LAUGHING.

Then one of the dinner ladies said, "Lass! If there was treasure in this school, trust me, we'd be the **FIRST** ones to find it!"

And they all laughed again for ages.

Then when Mr Graves eventually stopped laughing he said that we didn't need to be worrying about SCHOOL FUNDS – that was HIS job.

Then he said that the SCHOOL BUS SITUATION was

UNDER CONTROL

and that there was going to be a big FUNDRAISER soon and that he was CONFIDENT we'd raise enough money to get it fixed.

Then he looked at one of the dinner ladies and said, "Cheryl? Would you like to explain about the ketchup?"

And I looked at Jodi and she looked at me because Mr Graves had just called the dinner lady "CHERYL".

That's when the dinner lady said, "SUGAR. There's too much SUGAR in tomato ketchup. It's not healthy."

Gary

and I knew that it was because that meant

we weren't going to be getting the little packets of tomato ketchup back.

Then Gary said, "Why have you been giving us fewer chips? Can we have a fundraiser for more chips as well?"

And the dinner ladies all laughed and said, "It's only YOU, Mr Petrie, who's been getting fewer chips. Because you ask for them every day! Chips, chips and MORE chips! And if you don't watch yourself, you'll get NONE."

Gary didn't say anything after that because he obviously wanted to keep his chips.

Then Maisie asked about the HOLEY

CURTAINS and BROKEN TOILET SEAT and Mr Graves said, "Um, yes. One thing at a time."

And we all knew that that meant we didn't have enough money to get the bus AND new curtains, and that he wanted the BUS, and that was fair enough.

But then Jodi said, "Mr Graves, why didn't you tell Gary's dad it was your CAT'S EYES he'd seen shining behind the boiler?"

And that's when Mr Graves's face went a bit red and he said, "I didn't want anyone to know that I'd brought my cat into school with me. It's not really allowed."

And then Mr Graves gave Gary and Cheese and Onion a quick look, and I knew that it was because GARY had ALSO brought his cat into school and that he was probably going to get into BIG TROUBLE for it.

Then he said, "The dinner ladies caught me looking for TREASURE in the kitchen and made me tell them what I was doing."

I looked at the dinner ladies and they were all nodding, and I knew that Mr Graves must have told them RIGHT AWAY when they asked, and that we weren't the ONLY ones who were scared of the DINNER LADIES (and the OFFICE LADIES). Mr Graves was probably just as scared of them as we were!

Then Mr Graves said, "Treasure had a very early vet appointment and there wasn't time to take her home again before the start of the school day, so I planned to keep her in my office and take her home at lunchtime. But she escaped."

And that's when I realised that even HEAD TEACHERS have to follow the rules and that they can't bring their cats into school without CONSEQUENCES. (And, to be honest, I thought Mr Graves would have KNOWN better after the whole SNAKE THING, but that's another story.)

So that's when Gary gave Cheese and Onion to Maisie to hold and got down on his hands and knees next to Mr Graves and said, "I have a special trick."

We watched as Gary started WHISPERING into the gap, saying stuff like, "It's okey-dokey, laddy-lou. Come and see Gary-wary, Treasure-weasure. Don't be scared, my ickle-wickle baby-boo."

I did NOT think it was going to work, but then, all of a sudden, we heard a tiny MEOW.

Mr Graves gasped and said, "It's working! It's working! You're CALMING her! Keep going, Gary!"

So Gary kept using his RIDICULOUS CAT WHISPERER voice (and Jodi tried not to laugh) until the cat was almost out.

Then Gary looked at Mr Graves and said, "Stage two. I make them myself!"

And we watched as Gary took some little BISCUITS out of his pocket and laid them

down in a little trail near the gap and said,
"Cats love 'em!"

Then suddenly a TINY black-and-white cat
poked its head out and started MUNCHING
the first biscuit.

I looked at Mr Graves and he had TEARS
in his eyes.

But I knew that they were HAPPY TEARS

this time.

The little cat took another step forward and ate the next biscuit and then the next until she was completely out from behind the boiler.

That's when Gary gently picked her up while feeding her **ANOTHER** biscuit from his hand and then he placed her in Mr Graves's arms.

Then he gave Cheese and Onion a biscuit and a scratch on the head. And it was obvious that he did it because he didn't want Cheese and Onion to get **JEALOUS** of the other cat.

Everyone

CHEERED

and Gary did a **BOW** and Mr Graves cuddled Treasure while she munched away on Gary's homemade cat biscuits.

And then Gary bent down again and took off his **STINKY SHOE** and used it to reach Zach's phone.

Mr Graves and Zach **BOTH** kept thanking Gary over and over.

And that's when Gary reached up and put

his HAND on Mr Graves's shoulder and said, "Tell you what, if you REALLY want to thank me, why don't we just forget that you ever saw Cheese and Onion? Hmm?"

And Mr Graves went a bit red and then he said, "Who?" And then he smiled and we knew that that meant Gary wasn't in trouble for bringing a ninja cat to school.

But then suddenly Mr Graves's face CHANGED. And I thought that he'd CHANGED HIS MIND and that we were all about to get

EXPELLED

for the cat and for being in the basement. But then we all heard Treasure's tummy make a

LOUD
GURGLING SOUND.

And Mr Graves said, "Treasure! Was that you?!"

And all the dinner ladies started covering their mouths and noses and complaining about the STENCH.

And that's when Gary said, "Yeah. Um. Cats LOVE my homemade biscuits, but they DO give them a bit o' wind."

And then Cheese and Onion's tummy made a LOUD GURGLING SOUND too and we all covered our noses and burst out laughing.

Acknowledgements

Huge thanks to my brilliant editor,
Kirsty Stansfield. You're a genius!

Massive thanks to the wonderfully talented Tom
for the FANTASTIC illustrations!
I have one word (well, three): CHEESE AND ONION!!!

Thanks also to my wonderful agent, Becky Bagnell, for
always being there and for believing in me. I appreciate
every second of your time – thank you.

Most of all, thank you to my wee boy, Albie,
for inspiring me every day.
It was SO AMAZING having you with me on book tour.
Thank you for helping me sign my books (even though
you did also sign one by Axel Scheffler).
I can't wait for our next adventure together.
I love you x